For Mick
and in memory of my mum

First U.S. edition 2013

Library of Congress Catalog Card Number 2012942659

ISBN 978-0-7636-6241-7

13 14 15 16 17 18 TLF 10 9 8 7 6 5 4 3 2 1

Printed in Dongguan, Guangdong, China

This book was typeset in Aunt Mildred.
The illustrations were done in watercolor and pen.

Candlewick Press
99 Dover Street
Somerville, Massachusetts 02144

visit us at www.candlewick.com

BYE-BYE
BABY BROTHER!

Sheena Dempsey

CANDLEWICK PRESS

"What will we do now, Rory?" asked Ruby.

"I can't think of any more games to play."

Rory couldn't, either.

He was feeling a bit sleepy.

"Maybe Mom will know one.

Let's go find her!"

"Mom, will you come and play with us?"
Ruby asked. "We need a new game!"
"Oh, Ruby, I'd love to," said Mom,
"but I just need to change
Oliver's diaper."

So Ruby tried some hairdressing. Then she put Rory in a lovely blue sweater.

"Mr. Rory, you are beautiful," she said. "Let's show Mom!"

Mom thought Rory looked very handsome, but she was still too busy to play. "I just need to make Oliver's lunch," she said.

Grrrrrr . . .

So Ruby and Rory decided
to do some reading.
Rory was a very clever dog,
but he couldn't do
all the funny voices,
not like Mom.

"Mom, is it time to play yet?"

"Almost ready," she said.

"Let me finish feeding Oliver."

Ruby stomped outside.

"It's not fair. Mom's always taking
care of Oliver! Babies are so BORING!

If this stick was a magic wand . . .

I would make that baby disappear!

FIZZ-WHIZZ-POW!"

RUBY'S AMAZING MAGIC SHOW

LINE UP! LINE UP!

Marvel at the Vanishing Baby Act!

Where: The Kitchen   When: After lunch

Who: Ruby the Great and Her Lovely Assistant,
Rory the Dog

"Or maybe . . . when we go to
the supermarket, I could hide
Oliver in the cabbages.
Mom would never find him."

Woof!

"Or maybe I could sell Oliver in a yard sale. If we give him a good wash, I bet someone will buy him."

Then Ruby had her best idea yet.

"I could build a rocket and send

Oliver to the MOON — whoosh!

Then he'd really disappear."

So Ruby began to build the Magic Disappearing
Space Rocket. And Rory was a big help.

"There you are, Ruby! What's all this?" asked Mom.

"It's a rocket. I'm sending Oliver to
the moon," said Ruby.

"It's a lovely rocket," said Mom,
"but maybe Oliver is a bit small
to drive it. Could we all
go together?"

Ruby thought for a moment.
"OK . . ." she said, "but only
if I can be the captain."
"Of course you can,"
said Mom.
"LET'S GO!"
said Ruby.

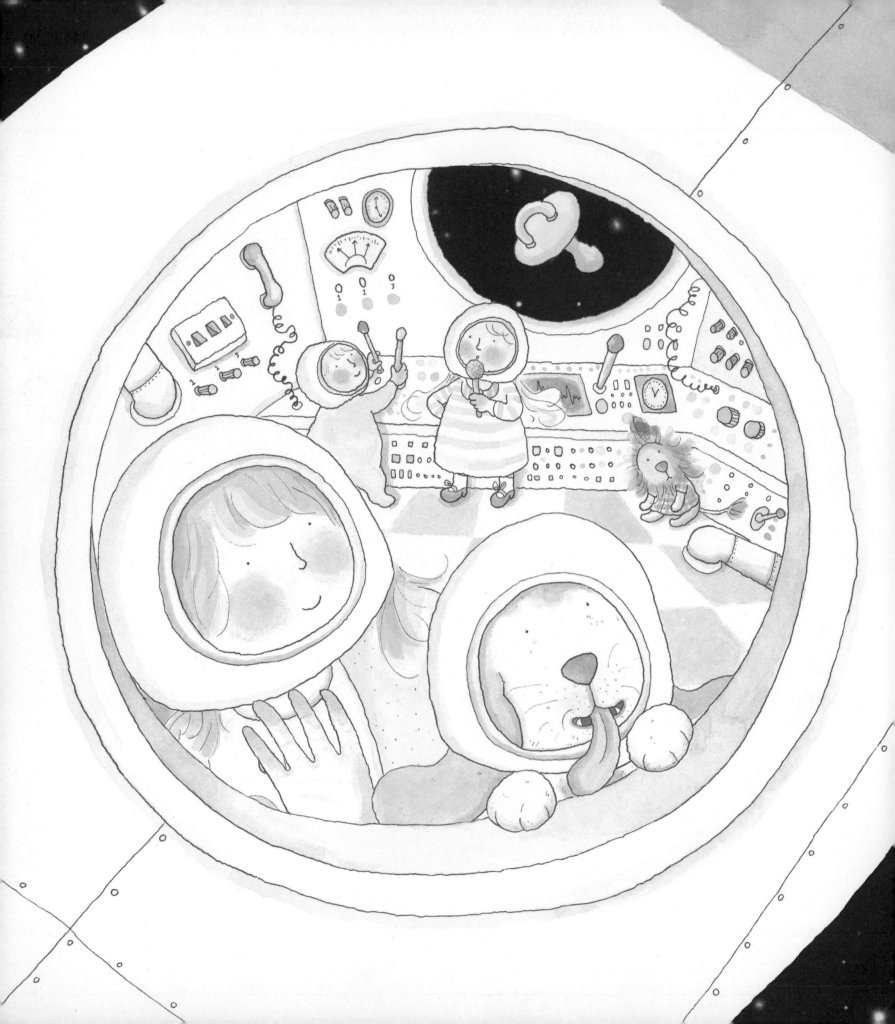

"This is your captain,
Ruby, speaking.
We are on our way
to the moon.
Please strap in
your baby and
hold on tight.
No drooling allowed."

It was the best space adventure they'd ever had and they got back just in time for bed. "Space travel is very tiring for little astronauts," said Mom. "Shall we get Oliver ready for his afternoon nap?"

Woof!

And so they did.

It was time to curl up for a story,
and Mom did all the funny voices,
just the way Ruby liked.

"Mom," said Ruby, "guess what."

"What?" said Mom.

"Today, I really wished Oliver
would disappear. But now . . .
I think we should keep him a little bit longer."

"Yes, let's," said Mom.
"I think Oliver
would like that."